ANIMALS OF THE OCEANS

Sharks

Susan Brocker

CONTENTS

INTRODUCTION

Sharks are probably the most feared creatures on earth. When we think of sharks, we think of huge jaws, sharp teeth, and staring eyes—little more than ferocious killing machines lurking in the depths of the oceans. But this is only part of the story. Some sharks are so gentle they will allow divers to hold onto their fins and take a ride.

Although sharks can be found in all the oceans of the world, they are most common in warmer waters. Some live in shallow bays or coral reefs, while others live in the deepest parts of the oceans.

Above: Our fear of sharks is summed up by the huge jaws of this great white shark.

A few even spend time in lakes and rivers, traveling regularly from salt to fresh water.

Sharks come in many different shapes and sizes and behave in many different ways. Whale sharks can weigh twice as much as an elephant, but the young of the spined pygmy shark are no bigger than your little finger. Some sharks are fierce hunters, while others drift placidly in the sea feeding on plankton.

As a group, sharks are very successful. They have few diseases and few enemies apart from other sharks and humans. As predators and scavengers, sharks are important in keeping the natural balance in the world's oceans.

Left: Whale sharks are gentle giants, allowing divers to play with them and to even hitch rides.

3

THE SHARK GROUP

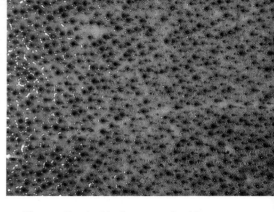

Sharks belong to a group of fish known as the Selasmobranchs, or cartilaginous fishes. Rays and skates also belong to this group. Most fish have a skeleton made of bones, but shark skeletons are made of a tough, rubbery material called cartilage.

Like other fish, sharks breathe through their gills. But whereas bony fish have a protective cover over their gills, sharks have gill slits. In most sharks, these gill slits can be seen on each side of the shark's head.

Unlike other fish, which have a gas-filled bag called a swim bladder to keep them afloat, sharks have a large liver filled with oil. The oil helps reduce the shark's weight in water and stops it from sinking.

Sharks do not have scales. Instead, their bodies are covered with tiny, toothlike

Above: Shark skin is covered with denticles, which give the skin its roughness. Dried shark skin, called shagreen, was used as sandpaper.

Left: Sharks breathe through their gill slits, which can be clearly seen on the side of this lemon shark's head.

4

points called denticles, which give the skin a rough texture. As sharks grow, the denticles fall off and are replaced by bigger ones.

There are more than four hundred different species of shark, and new species are being identified all the time. Of this huge number, only about thirty species have been known to attack people. Most sharks are completely harmless, including the two biggest: the whale shark and the basking shark.

Above: Some sharks have to swim continuously to stay afloat, or spend periods resting on the ocean floor; but many have large, oily livers for buoyancy.

WHALE and BASKING SHARKS

Above: The whale shark has a checkerboard pattern of spots on its skin.

The largest shark—and the largest fish in the world—is the whale shark. It can grow up to fifty feet long. The second largest shark is the basking shark, at about

6

Right: Basking sharks feed simply by cruising along with their mouths open and filtering plankton-rich water through their gills.

Below: The whale shark has numerous minute teeth which can hardly be seen in the vastness of its mouth.

thirty-three feet long. They are harmless, gentle giants, feeding on tiny animals called plankton that float in the sea.

Both sharks are filter-feeders. They scoop up huge quantities of water in their broad mouths and, as the water passes through their gills, strain the food out in special filters.

The whale shark is massive, with a gigantic, flattened head and a vast, straight mouth. As well as feeding on plankton, whale sharks sometimes feed on small fish. They rise up vertically through schools of fish, catching the fish in their gaping mouths.

Basking sharks often swim languidly along the surface of the water as if basking in the sun. In fact, they are skimming the top layer of the sea for plankton. Basking sharks are easily identified by their enormous gill slits, which almost completely encircle their necks.

7

OTHER HARMLESS SHARKS

Most close encounters with sharks occur without people even realizing they have happened. Well before a diver has a chance to notice a shark, it has already hidden or fled. The majority of sharks have far more to fear from us than we have to fear from them. All sharks, however, should be treated with respect.

A good example of a usually harmless shark is the nurse shark. Nurse sharks live in warm, shallow waters and can grow up to fifteen feet long. They have broad heads, stout bodies, and are sluggish, spending most of their time lying on the seabed feeding on shellfish. Although nurse sharks do not attack people, they will defend themselves if harassed and can give a nasty bite.

Many other sharks, like the numerous species of cat sharks and dogfish sharks, go about their lives without bothering people. Some have slanted eyes and colorful patterns of spots or stripes just like

8

cats. Dogfish sharks range from the tiniest sharks to giants like the sleeper dogfish that can grow to twenty-three feet.

Because they looked fierce, sand tigers or gray nurse sharks were often blamed for attacks on people, and many were slaughtered. But it's now known that these sharks are inoffensive creatures, and in New South Wales they are protected. It seems that in the shark world appearances can be deceiving.

9

Left: Ever since the movie *Jaws*, the great white shark has had a reputation as a bloodthirsty killer.

GREAT WHITE and TIGER SHARKS

Of the thrity or so species of shark that have been known to attack people, the great white, the tiger, and the bull have been blamed for causing the most deaths and injuries. Mako and hammerhead sharks are also known to attack humans.

Perhaps none inspires more fear than the great white shark, also known as the white pointer or even white death. It has come to symbolize everything people fear about sharks. It is big, powerful, and terrible to behold, with gaping jaws, jagged teeth, and pitch black eyes.

The great white is the largest and strongest predatory fish in the sea. Great whites can grow up to thirty feet long. They live in cool to tropical waters and prey on sea mammals, big fish, and other sharks.

The great white is the only fish that has the spine-chilling habit of silently lifting its head out of the water as if to investigate where its next meal is coming from. Many fishermen have had the feeling they were being watched, only to discover the eyes of a great white upon them.

The second most dangerous shark in the world is the tiger shark. It gets its name from the dark body stripes on the sides of the

younger sharks. Tiger sharks are easily recognized by their broad heads, blunt snouts, and large mouths. They live mainly in tropical waters and can grow up to sixteen feet long. Tiger sharks are sometimes called the garbage cans of the sea because they will eat anything and everything, including animal carcasses, rubbish thrown overboard from ships, and even tin cans and car tires.

Right: Tiger sharks use their serrated teeth to tear chunks off large prey, or simply swallow smaller prey whole.

OTHER DANGEROUS SHARKS

Bull sharks live in shallow, tropical seas, but are also one of the few shark species that spend time in fresh water. They often swim far up warm rivers such as the Amazon, and have even been found in the Mississippi River in the United States.

Heavy-bodied and stout, bull sharks can grow to about eleven feet long. Like tiger sharks, they are aggressive feeders and will eat almost anything.

Mako sharks are the fastest in the sea, and a favorite among game fishermen. When hooked on a line, makos will fight by leaping clear out of the water, so high that they sometimes land on the decks of fishing boats. They have also been known to attack the hulls of boats.

Left: The speed, power, and sharp teeth of the mako shark make it a potential danger to divers.

12

Mako sharks live in warm and tropical waters and reach a length of eleven feet. They have fanglike teeth for grabbing large fish, such as mackerel and herrings, and will even tackle swordfish.

Hammerheads are the oddest looking of the dangerous sharks. Their heads protrude out from their bodies like the heads of hammers. Their eyes and nostrils are at the tips of the hammerhead, sometimes at a distance of up to twenty-three inches apart.

Above: Bull sharks have killed people in rivers and inland lakes such as Lake Nicaragua.

Only the bigger species of hammerhead shark, like the great hammerhead, which can grow to sixteen feet, have been known to attack humans. Generally, hammerheads are timid sharks and only approach divers to steal speared fish from them.

Left: Hammerheads have very good eyesight. They can see all around because their eyes are set on the tips of their heads.

13

WEIRD SHARKS

The world's most unusual shark, the megamouth, wasn't even discovered until 1976. Megamouth means big mouth, and that's exactly what it is. The toothless grin of the huge shark can measure up to three feet across, while the rest of the body is about sixteen feet long. They are tropical, deep-sea filter-feeders.

Below: The head and mouth of a wobbegong sport whiskers that look like trailing seaweed.

One of the ugliest sharks is the goblin shark. It has a long, pointed dagger for a snout; jaws that protrude when feeding with needle-sharp teeth; tiny eyes; and a flabby body. Goblin sharks reach a length of about ten feet and live in the deep sea. Not a lot is known about them, though it is thought they feed on prey such as shrimp and small fish.

Horn sharks get their name from the two spines that stick out on their backs. They are also called bullhead sharks or pig sharks because they have blunt heads with squashed-in snouts and big nostrils. Horn sharks grow to five feet and live on the

seabed, feeding on shellfish and small fish.

Wobbegongs also live on the ocean floor and have flattened bodies. They are masters of camouflage, and hide in the hollows of rocky reefs waiting for prey such as crabs to stumble by. Their ornate disguises include spotted or striped skins, and tassels or frills on their heads that look like beards of seaweed. They grow up to ten feet long.

Above: The Port Jackson shark is a species of horn shark. It is very fond of oysters, which it crushes up with its blunt back teeth.

Below: Very few goblin sharks have been seen alive. Scientists learned of their existence from carcasses brought up in deep-sea fishing nets.

SHARK RELATIVES

Rays and skates, including the guitarfish and the sawfish, belong to the same group of fish as sharks. To look at them, you wouldn't think so. They are broad and flattened in shape, with eyes on the tops of their heads and gills and mouths on their bellies. But they all have skeletons made of cartilage, just like the sharks.

Above: The colorful blue spotted ray is easily camouflaged against a backdrop of bright coral.

Right: The graceful manta ray is broader than it is long.

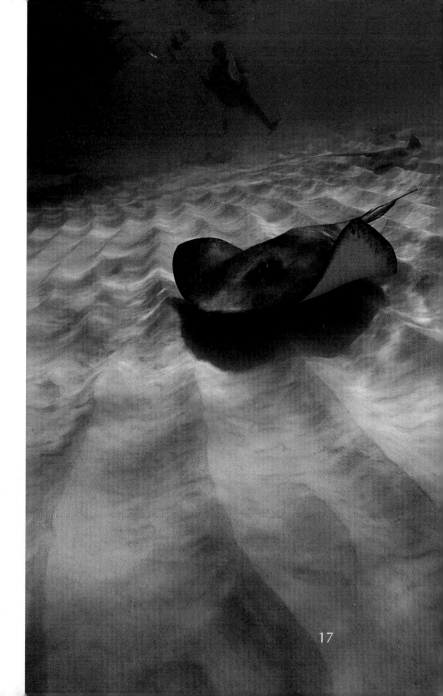

The most distinctive feature of many rays and skates are the winglike fins on the sides of their bodies. They look as if they are flying through the water as they use their wings to propel themselves. Giant manta rays have enormous wings and can measure up to twenty-three feet across. They are harmless filter-feeders like whale sharks and basking sharks.

Most rays and skates live on the seabed, where they feed on small fish and shellfish. They are cleverly patterned with spots or blotches, which make them difficult to see against the rocks and coral. Sometimes they even bury themselves in the sand to lie in wait for their prey.

Some rays have developed protective devices for defense against their enemies. Stingrays are armed with poisonous, saw-toothed spines on their tails. Electric rays have organs on each side of their heads that can deliver shocks of up to 200 volts.

Right: People wading in shallow water where stingrays live should tread carefully, as the rays have been found in water less than four inches deep.

THE SHARK'S BODY

Sharks are among one of the most successful predators on earth, and one of the oldest. Sharks lived three hundred and fifty million years ago, and have remained largely unchanged for the past seventy million years. Their success is due to a variety of adaptations to a predatory lifestyle in the sea.

A shark's skeleton of cartilage is lighter and more elastic than that of a bony fish, enabling it to swim with ease. The tiny,

Below: The body of the gray reef shark is that of a typical shark: streamlined and powerful.

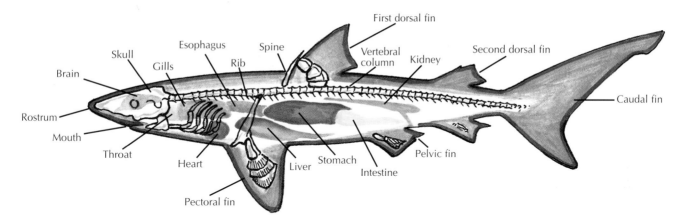

First dorsal fin

Esophagus

Spine

Skull

Gills

Rib

Vertebral column

Kidney

Second dorsal fin

Brain

Rostrum

Mouth

Throat

Heart

Pectoral fin

Liver

Stomach

Intestine

Pelvic fin

Caudal fin

Above: Diagram of a shark's body.

toothlike denticles on the shark's skin are backward-pointing and help channel the water and reduce drag.

The shape of a shark's body depends upon the life it leads. Aggressive hunters have a torpedo-shaped body and a powerful tail. This streamlined shape helps them move swiftly through the water after prey. The more sluggish, bottom-dwelling sharks have flexible, tapered bodies suited to hiding out among the coral and rocks in wait for prey.

Most sharks have two fins on their backs (dorsal fins), two sets of fins on their sides (pectoral fins and pelvic fins), and a smaller fin on the undersides of their bodies.

Above: The propulsive movement of the shark's tail can be seen as this blue shark swims away.

BREATHING and MOVING

Sharks get oxygen from the water through their gills. The gills open to the outside through slits— usually five, but sometimes six or seven. Many sharks cannot pump water over their gills as most fish are able to do. They must swim constantly to force water through their mouths and over their gills.

Sharks are powerful and graceful swimmers. They propel themselves through the water by waving their tails from side to side. The fins help sharks to balance, steer, and brake in the water. Some sharks that live on the sea floor, such as horn sharks, can use their fins to crawl along the bottom.

Like body shape, different shark species have differently shaped tails according to their lifestyles. The mako shark has a crescent-shaped tail, which helps it attain great speeds. The thresher shark has a tail that is almost as long

Left: Most sharks breathe through five gill slits, but the seven-gilled shark has two extra slits.

20

as the rest of its body and shaped like a huge scythe. It uses its tail to quickly round up and stun its prey.

Most of the time, sharks swim leisurely, cruising slowly through the water. But they are also capable of incredible bursts of speed and can mount lightning attacks on unsuspecting prey. In a sprint, the mako shark can reach speeds of over 21.7 miles an hour.

Above: The longer upper tail lobe of the sand tiger shark helps it achieve sudden bursts of speed.

Right: The wobbegong uses its tail to swim with an eel-like motion.

21

FEEDING

All sharks are carnivores or meat eaters. Different species of shark feed on different things, from plankton to sea lions. Some sharks, like the tiger and bull sharks, will eat almost anything.

Depending on what type of food sharks eat, they have different kinds of teeth. The smooth dogfish shark has strong, flat teeth for crushing crabs; the sand tiger has long, hooked teeth for snaring fish; and the tiger shark has enormous, serrated teeth for tearing off chunks of meat from large prey.

Sharks never run out of teeth. They can have from three to fifteen rows of them. When the front teeth break or wear out, new ones from the row behind take their places. The new teeth

Left: During feeding frenzies, the smell of blood in the water excites sharks and they become increasingly aggressive.

Left: The whale shark's large mouth and minute teeth are adapted for filter-feeding.

Below: The tiger shark is able to tear chunks off its prey using its sharp teeth.

form in the gums and roll forward when they are needed, like a conveyor belt of teeth. Every ten days or two weeks, the shark's teeth are completely replaced. Shark teeth are often found stuck in the flesh of their prey.

The jaws of certain sharks are only loosely attached to the rest of the skull, so they can thrust their jaws forward and their snouts back to get an easy grip on their prey with their teeth.

Some sharks indulge in eating orgies known as feeding frenzies. Large numbers of sharks home in on the same prey and become over-excited. The sea soon becomes a writhing mass of snapping, slashing, tearing jaws, as the sharks attack the prey, each other, and anything else that might get in the way.

SHARK SENSES

Like people, sharks can smell, see, hear, taste, and touch. They also have unique senses which help them survive in the sea. Some species, for example, migrate hundreds of miles across the oceans. They are able to navigate using their own internal compasses, which are sensitive to the earth's magnetic field.

The sharks' sense of smell is acute. They can pick up the faintest scent of blood or body fluids from a distance of more than half a mile away. The smells waft to the shark on ocean currents, forming an odor corridor which the shark follows upstream to its prey.

Right: The small pits on the shark's snout are sensory pores that help the shark pick up electrical currents made by its prey.

Scientists once called sharks "swimming noses," believing that their incredible sense of smell made up for poor eyesight. But they discovered that most sharks have eyes that are especially adapted to see in the dim light of the oceans. The fast-moving sharks, in particular, make use of sight for hunting.

When it comes to low-pitched sounds, sharks have excellent hearing. They can hear and locate low-frequency sounds in the water, exactly the sort made by wounded prey. Fishermen on Pacific islands traditionally shook coconut rattles underwater to attract sharks.

Sharks have a special sense known as distant touch. A sensing line of nerves, called the lateral line, runs along each side of the shark's body and onto its head. This helps the shark to detect vibrations made by prey moving in the water. Small pores on the shark's nose, known as Ampullae of Lorenzini, also detect weak electric signals produced by prey.

Above: In bottom-dwelling species, such as the wobbegong, eyesight is not as important as it is to the open-sea hunters.

Right: Diagram of the shark's lateral line.

LIFE CYCLE

Many species of shark live in different parts of the ocean according to their size and sex. When it comes to finding a mate, they may travel to special breeding grounds. Here the male and female play a game of cat and mouse, where the male tries to bite the female to encourage mating. It looks fierce, but females have tougher skins than the males.

Unlike most fish, sharks fertilize their eggs internally. The male shark has two organs, called claspers, attached to the pelvic fins, which channel sperm into the female to fertilize the eggs. In most species, the fertilized eggs develop inside the female, and she gives birth to live baby sharks called pups.

Some species lay their eggs outside their bodies. Nurse sharks can even choose, depending on which method is best suited to conditions at the time. Shark eggs are often encased in leathery shells with dangling tendrils that secure them to seaweed and rocks.

Below: It is very common for female sharks to bear the scars from mating games.

26

Some sharks may have more than one hundred and thirty pups, but most have fewer than thirty. The sand tiger shark produces only two young. Once a mother has given birth she swims off, leaving the pups to their own devices. They are fully developed and able to care for themselves. Some sharks give their offspring a good start in life by birthing in nurseries where the water is warm, safe from other sharks, and full of small fish to eat.

Above: Some baby sharks develop inside their mothers or egg cases, but are nourished by a yolk sac. This pup still has its yolk sac attached.

Below: Sharks are usually loners, seldom coming together to do anything other than mate. Hammerhead sharks are an exception, as they often group together in large schools.

27

SHARK ATTACK!

Fewer than one hundred shark attacks are reported around the world each year. About twenty-five to thirty of these result in death. That's a small number, considering the number of swimmers, divers, and surfers who enter into shark territory.

Scientists think that some shark attacks are due to mistaken identity. From beneath the water a person swimming, diving, or surfing may look like a seal to a hungry shark. This seems to be supported by the fact that many victims are spat out after the first bite. Sharks may also attack if they feel threatened or teased.

People should apply common sense when entering the water in areas known to have sharks. Always take heed of warning notices or advice. Swim or dive with a companion and avoid murky water. Don't swim or dive with an open wound or where bait has been put out, as

Left: Underwater photographers take photographs of dangerous sharks from the safety of specially designed shark cages.

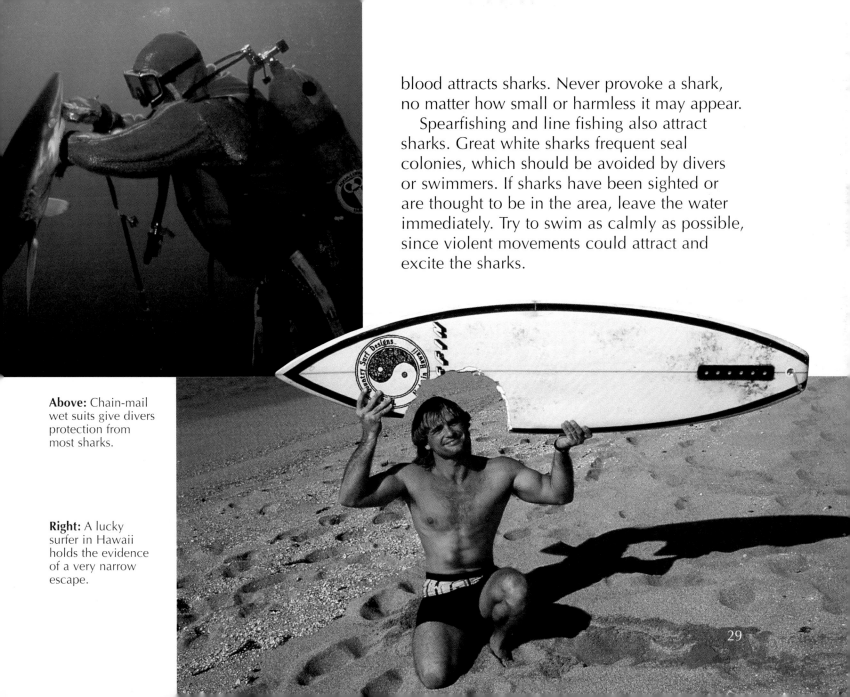

blood attracts sharks. Never provoke a shark, no matter how small or harmless it may appear.

Spearfishing and line fishing also attract sharks. Great white sharks frequent seal colonies, which should be avoided by divers or swimmers. If sharks have been sighted or are thought to be in the area, leave the water immediately. Try to swim as calmly as possible, since violent movements could attract and excite the sharks.

Above: Chain-mail wet suits give divers protection from most sharks.

Right: A lucky surfer in Hawaii holds the evidence of a very narrow escape.

29

SHARKS and PEOPLE

Sharks are useful to people in many different ways. Their meat is eaten or used for fertilizer; their fins are made into soup; their skin is used to make leather goods; their teeth are made into jewelry and decorations; and oil from their livers is used in industry and cosmetics.

Often sharks are killed needlessly. Sharks are caught in huge numbers in commercial fishing nets and are often thrown back into the sea dead. Sport fishing for sharks has become increasingly popular, the jaws of large sharks like the great white being the ultimate prize.

There is a danger that we are slaughtering too many sharks. The future of some species is already at risk. But while it's easy to drum up sympathy for the friendly dolphin and whale, not many people care about the plight of the shark.

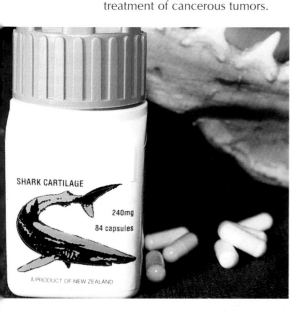

Below: Some recent scientific research suggests that shark cartilage extracts may help in the treatment of cancerous tumors.

Right: The jaws and teeth of large sharks are valued by trophy hunters.

30

Fortunately, conservationists are now recognizing the importance of sharks in the ecology of the oceans. In some places around the world, the fishing of certain shark species is banned; there are limits on the number of sharks that can be killed; and sharks are protected in special marine reserves.

Above: Traditional swords from Tuvalu in the Pacific are made from shark teeth and coconut wood.

Left: Every year countless numbers of sharks die entangled in fishing nets.

31

INDEX

First published in 1997 by David Bateman Ltd.,
30 Tarndale Grove, Albany Business Park,
Albany, Auckland, New Zealand

Copyright © David Bateman Ltd., 1997

First edition for the United States and Canada
published by Barron's Educational Series, Inc., 1997

Text: Susan Brocker, B.A.
Editorial consultant: Malcolm Francis, M.Sc.
Photographs: Malcolm Francis, Key-Light Image Library,
Natural Images, New Zealand Picture Library, Clive Roberts
(Museum of New Zealand), Sea Watch Foundation, Robert
Suisted, Kim Westerskov
Illustrations: Caren Glazer
Design: Errol McLeary

All inquiries should be addressed to:
Barron's Educational Series, Inc.
250 Wireless Boulevard
Hauppauge, New York 11788

Library of Congress Catalog Card No. 97-19632
International Standard Book No. 0-7641-0260-5

Library of Congress Cataloging-in-Publication Data
Brocker, Susan, 1961–
    Sharks / Susan Brocker.
        p. cm. — (Animals of the oceans)
        Originally published: Auckland, N.Z. : D. Bateman
        Ltd., 1995.
        Includes index.
        Summary: Describes the physical characteristics,
    habits, and natural environment of various species of
    perhaps the most feared creatures on earth.
        ISBN 0-7641-0260-5
        1. Sharks—Juvenile literature. [1. Sharks.] I. Title.
    II. Series.
    QL638.9B74 1997
    597.3—dc21   97-19632
                                                            CIP
                                                            AC
Printed in Hong Kong
9 8 7 6 5 4 3 2 1